Jag's
New Friend

Special thanks to Jan Miles

Library of Congress Cataloging-in-Publication Data
Rimes, LeAnn.
Jag's new friend/by LeAnn Rimes; illustrated by Richard Bernal—1st ed.
p. cm.
Summary: Feeling neglected by her friends, Jag the jaguar starts spending time
with a snake name Bo but soon realizes that he is not as cool as he seemed
and she has put her friend Isabel the parrot in danger.
ISBN 0-525-47298-3
[1. Friendship—Fiction. 2. Jaguars—Fiction. 3. Snakes—Fiction. 4. Parrots—Fiction.
5. Animals—Fiction] I. Bernal, Richard, ill. II. Title.
PZ7.R458 Jag 2004
[E]—dc22   2003023635

Published in the United States by Dutton Children's Books,
a division of Penguin Young Readers Group
345 Hudson Street, New York, New York 10014
www.penguin.com

Printed in China • First Edition
1 3 5 7 9 10 8 6 4 2

LeAnn Rimes

Jag's New Friend

STORY DEVELOPED BY DEAN SHEREMET

ILLUSTRATED BY RICHARD BERNAL

A Byron Preiss Book

DUTTON CHILDREN'S BOOKS • NEW YORK

The clouds floated like lily pads on a river-blue sky.

"That long one looks like an alligator," said Simon, pointing.

"It does," Jag agreed. "And the little ones under it look like fish."

As they lay in the grass, the sun began to set. Jag was happily wiggling her toes in the warmth when Simon jumped up. "It's late!" he declared. "I have to get to practice."

"Practice?!" exclaimed Jag. "But it's Saturday."

"I know," Simon said with a shrug, "but we have a big meet coming up. Besides, you don't get to be captain of the climbing team by lying around looking at clouds. See you later!"

And with that, he sped into the forest,
leaving Jag to find her own fun.

By Monday after school, Jag was a little tired of being by herself. Making angels in the grass wasn't as much fun without a friend to see them. And the snail races she had set up on Sunday were still going nowhere slowly.

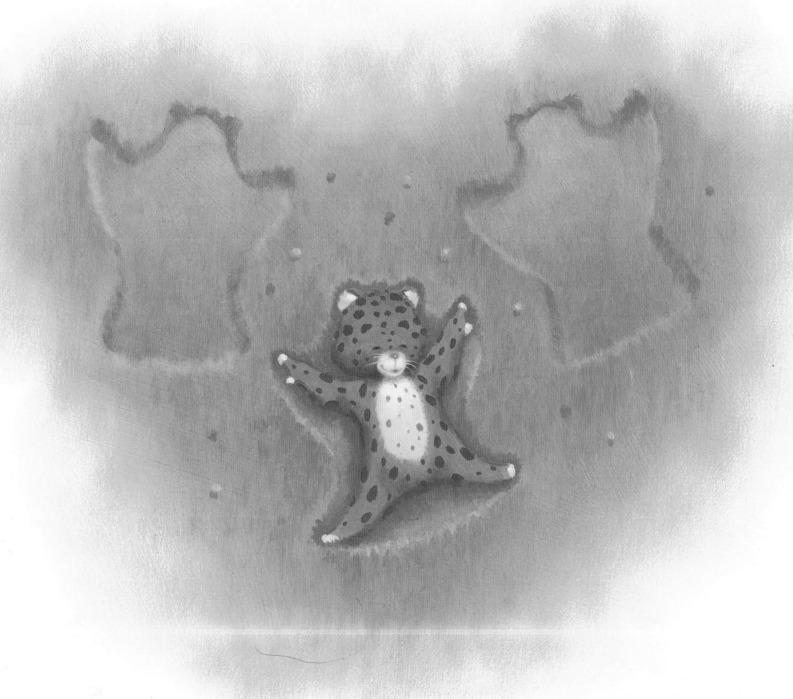

But Simon had to practice again with his teammates, who shifted impatiently from foot to foot as they waited for him. "Maybe tomorrow," said Simon, and he hurried away from her again.

With a snort and a growl, Jag stomped away home.

"You're here early," her mother said.

"Simon never has time for me anymore," Jag whined. "So I don't have anybody to play with."

"Well, that can't be true," her mother replied. "What about your friend Isabel? Maybe you should pay her a visit." Jag's mother headed toward the door, patting Jag on the head. "In the meantime, I have to run out and get a few more things for dinner."

And then Jag was all alone again.

So with a heavy sigh, Jag headed out of the cave to visit Isabel the parrot.

She climbed the tree, only to find that Isabel was not home. Lately it seemed like she was hardly ever home. "I guess I shouldn't be surprised," Jag grumbled.

She was still muttering to herself when she heard, "Sssssssay, what sssseems to be the problem?"

Jag looked up to see who was talking. When she saw him, she frowned and said, "Oh. Simon says not to speak to snakes."

The snake looked offended. "Ssssimon sssaysss . . . Do you believe everything Ssssimon sssaysss?"

"Well, actually . . ."

"Never mind. Don't anssswer that. But do tell me what'sss the matter. Perhapsss I can help."

Jag thought for a moment. Her mom was busy. Isabel wasn't home. And Simon never had time for her anyway, so why not talk to the snake?

Nobody else cared.

"Well," said Jag, "nobody has time for me anymore."

"My goodnesss!" said the snake. "No time for you? Why, they probably aren't cool enough for you anyway. But who is cooler than a sssnake? Here, feel!" he exclaimed, dropping his tail down for Jag to touch. It was indeed cool.

"I'm Bo," he said. Jag introduced herself and shook Bo's tail. "Now what shall we do first?"

Jag's fur tingled, and she declared, "Angels in the grass!" So Jag made angels, and Bo made bow ties in the meadow. Then they tracked the progress of Jag's snail races. Bo even challenged her to a tree-climbing race, which she won easily.

"Now that we're friendsss, I have another game," Bo hissed. "Come thisss way."

Jag followed Bo to an unfamiliar tree, and they climbed high into its branches before stopping.

"All you have to do is ssstay here on thisss branch while I go over to that one." Bo pointed vaguely with his tail. "And, just to prove that we're loyal friends to the end, if you sssee or hear anyone coming, give a sssignal, like thisss." Bo put his tongue between his teeth and whistled. "Can you do that?"

Jag threw her shoulders back and gave her new best friend a mock salute. "Aye, aye, Captain," she said, grinning.

"Sssuper!" said Bo, and away he slinked.

Jag sat on the branch feeling smug. She had found a new friend. And to think, Simon had told her snakes weren't cool!

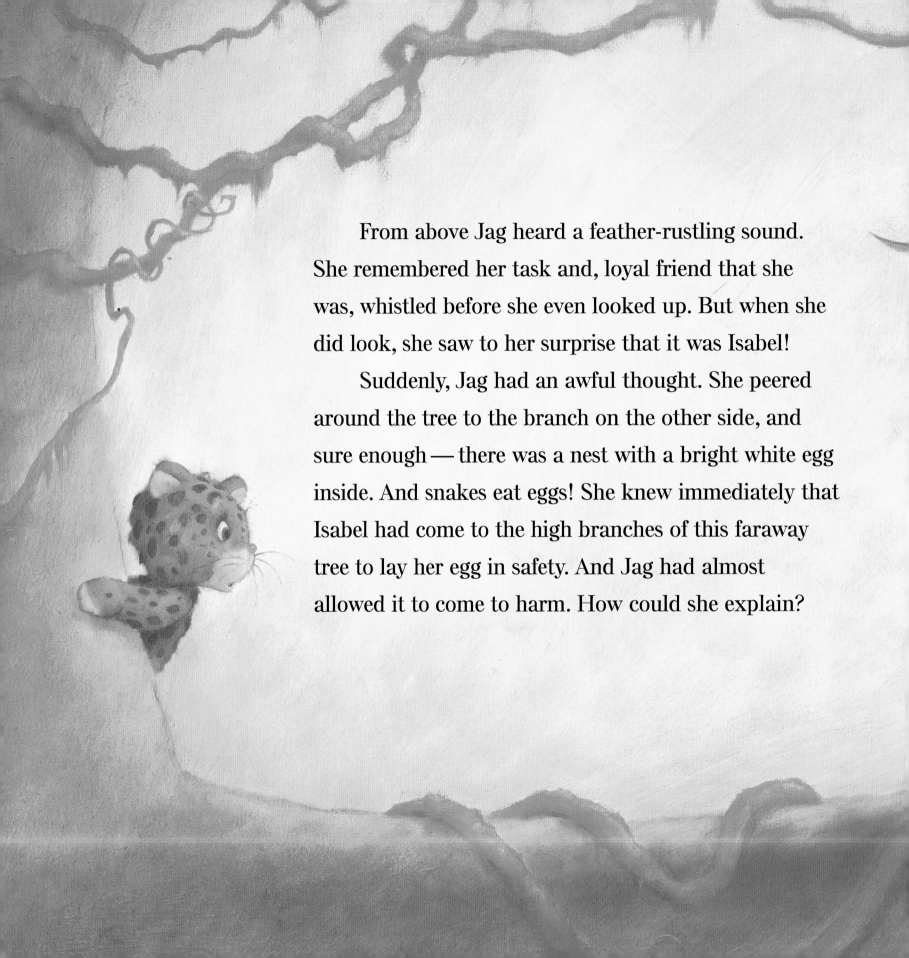

From above Jag heard a feather-rustling sound. She remembered her task and, loyal friend that she was, whistled before she even looked up. But when she did look, she saw to her surprise that it was Isabel!

Suddenly, Jag had an awful thought. She peered around the tree to the branch on the other side, and sure enough — there was a nest with a bright white egg inside. And snakes eat eggs! She knew immediately that Isabel had come to the high branches of this faraway tree to lay her egg in safety. And Jag had almost allowed it to come to harm. How could she explain?

Bo was slithering swiftly away
from the nest, and all Jag could think of
was to run away, too. So that's exactly
what she did.

That night, Jag fidgeted her way
through dinner. "What's the matter?"
her mother asked.

"Nothing," Jag mumbled.

She fidgeted her way
through class the next day.
"What's the problem?" asked
her teacher.

"Nothing," Jag replied.

All through lunch she was out
of sorts until Simon, who had been eating
with his teammates, approached her.
"What's going on?" asked Simon.

This time she scowled and responded, "Like you care! You're too busy to care. 'Maybe tomorrow'" — she mocked him — "maybe tomorrow you'll have time to care!"

And with that, she jumped up from the table and left him standing there alone.

After school, Jag was skulking her way toward home, looking rather ferocious. With only a slight hesitation, Simon stepped into her path.

"I have practice right now," Simon said to Jag, "but I wanted to come tell you something first." Jag crossed her arms over her chest and snarled, but Simon continued. "I understand why you're upset with me — I've been neglecting you. I should have made time for you. I'm sorry."

Despite herself, Jag felt her snarl turning into a smile. The apology made her feel much better. Then Simon added, "Say, maybe you and I can go visit Isabel after my practice today?"

"Isabel!" Jag exclaimed. And she knew exactly what she had to do. "Thank you for the apology," she said to Simon, "but I have to go see Isabel right now."

"Is something wrong?" Simon asked.

Jag nodded solemnly.

"Well, in that case, I'll come with you,"
he said. "I can miss a little practice — after
all, I am your best friend."

Jag felt braver right away.

So they went, arm-in-arm, into the
forest. Jag took Simon to the unfamiliar tree
with the nest way up high in its branches.
Simon agreed to wait for her at the bottom,
and Jag took a deep breath and climbed up.

When Isabel saw her, she crossed her wings over her chest and scowled. Jag knew just how she felt. Bravely, she cleared her throat and started to explain. "You see . . . it was a mistake," she said. "What happened was . . . well, no one was ever around to be my friend anymore. And then the snake . . . he said he'd be my friend. But I didn't know what he was doing . . . and then . . ."

Here Jag finally stopped,
took a deep breath, looked Isabel
in the eye, and said, "I'm so sorry."

After a few moments of silence, Isabel said, "I understand, Jag. But everyone can't pay attention to you all the time. Sometimes we will be busy with other things. And at those times, you can't just go hanging around with snakes. I hope you learned your lesson."

"I did!" Jag exclaimed. "The hard way. I almost ruined my chance of being a big sister!" Jag patted the egg in the nest and smiled at Isabel — who uncrossed her wings and smiled back at her.